Around the City

The Bank Street Readers

Prepared by the
Bank Street College of Education

SENIOR EDITOR *Irma Simonton Black*

MANAGING EDITOR *Carl Memling*

ASSOCIATE EDITORS *Joan W. Blos* *Betty Miles*

SKILLS CONSULTANT *Frances M. Kerr*

Formerly Senior Consultant
Reading Improvement Program
Board of Education
City of New York

Bank Street College of Education

Around the City

Illustrated by

Aurelius Battaglia
Mamoru Funai
David Klein
George Mocniak
June Otani

THE MACMILLAN COMPANY, NEW YORK
COLLIER-MACMILLAN LIMITED, LONDON

Contents

Part One

Part Two

© Copyright The Macmillan Company 1965

THE MACMILLAN COMPANY, NEW YORK
COLLIER-MACMILLAN CANADA, LTD., TORONTO, ONTARIO

Printed in the United States of America. 1 I

Part Three

Part Four

Acknowledgment

"One Potato, Two Potatoes," adapted from the book
Believe and Make-Believe, edited by Lucy Sprague Mitchell
and Irma Simonton Black. Copyright, ©, 1956, by the Bank
Street College of Education. Adapted by permission of E. P.
Dutton & Co., Inc.

Part One

All Around the City

All around the city,
All around the town,
Boys and girls run up the street.
Boys and girls run down.

Boys come out into the sun.
Boys come out to play and run.

Girls come out to run and play,
Around the city, all the day.

All around the city,
All around the town,
Boys and girls run up the street.
Boys and girls run down.

10

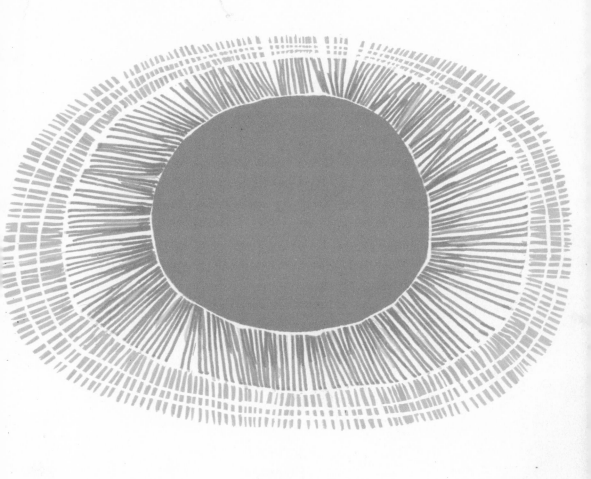

A Hot Day

It is hot.

The sun is high in the sky.
The sun is hot.

The street is hot.

The boys and girls sit down.
They sit on the steps.

It is a hot, hot day.

A truck comes down the street.
It is a water truck.

A boy runs out into the water.
He is cool.
The truck goes away.

A girl sits on the steps.
It is hot.

A man comes.
He turns the water on.

Girls go in the water.
Boys run in!
Boys and girls play in the water.

It is cool!

The street is cool.
The boys and girls are cool.

But the sun is hot.
The sun is hot, high in the sky.

Who Likes Ice Cream?

Who likes ice cream?
Who? Who?

I like ice cream.
Yes, I do.

She likes ice cream, too.

Do you like ice cream?

Yes, I do.
He likes ice cream, too.

I like ice cream.
Yes, I do.
The dog likes ice cream, too.

Boys like ice cream.
Girls like ice cream.
Dogs like ice cream, too!

Come and Jump

Jump, jump, jump!

One, one,
Have some fun.

Two, two,
I see you.

Three, three,
Look at me!

You like red.
I do, too.
You like me,
And I like you.

Jump, jump, jump!

Will Ben Get a Ride?

Ben is up in the house.
He sees a red truck on the street.
The truck stops.

Ben says, "Boy! A ride!"

20

A man jumps down from the truck.
"Come and ride," says the man.
"Come one, come all.
Have fun.
Get a ride!"

Boys and girls run to the truck.

The boys and girls jump up.
They ride around and around.
Slow, slow, slow.

They go around fast!
Fast, fast, fast!

Ben looks down.
He sees the boys and girls.

The boys and girls jump down.

"Get a ride," the man says.
"Come one, come all.
Have fun."

Ben sees it all from his house.
He sees all the fun.
"I will get a ride, too," says Ben.

Ben comes down from his house.
One step.
Two steps.
Three steps.

The ride stops.
"Good-by," says the man.
"I have to go away."

The man jumps up on his truck.
Ben comes down the street.
One step, two steps, three steps.

A girl turns around.
She sees Ben.
"Stop!" says the girl to the man.

All the boys and girls turn around.
"Stop!" they all say.

26

The man stops.
The man says, "Come on.
Come and get a ride."

Ben goes around and around.
Slow, slow, slow.
Fast, fast, fast!

Ben rides!

After School

After school,
What do you do?

I go to the store.
Do you go, too?

I read books.
What do you do?

I play with my dog.
What do you do?

I work with my mother.
Do you work, too?

I work with my father.
What do you do?

I play with my friends.
Do you play, too?

I look at TV.
Do you look, too?

After school,
What do you do?

Part Two

Fire Drill

RING! RING! RING!
It is a fire drill!

All the boys and girls come out.

Shhhhhhhh!

Little boys and girls come out.
Big boys and girls come out.
They all come down the school steps.

Shhhhhhhh!

Boys and girls go down the street.

Shhhhhhh!
Shhhhhhh!
The big boys and girls do not talk.
The little boys and girls do not talk.

34

RING! RING! RING!

Now the boys and girls come back.
They come back up the street.

Then they all go up the school steps.
The boys and girls do not talk.

Little girls and boys go in.
Then big boys and girls go in.
They all go in.

Now they are back in the rooms.

The fire drill is over.

Talk! Talk! Talk!
Talk! Talk! Talk! Talk!

The Day It Rained

One day it rained and rained.
It rained all day.

Carmen could not go out.

But still—
She went to see her friend.

It rained and rained.
Carmen could not go out.

But still—
Carmen could go to the mail box.

It rained all day.
Carmen could not go out.

But still——
Carmen went to do the wash.

It rained, and it rained.
Carmen could not go out.

But still——
She went to see her grandmother.

It rained, and it rained.
Carmen could not go out.

But still—
She went to get some milk.

It rained and rained.
It rained all day.
Carmen did not go out.

But still—
She went to see her friend.
She went to the mail box.

She did the wash with her mother.
She went to see her grandmother.
She went to get some milk.
　　Carmen went all around.
　　And she did not get wet!

The ABC

Who can do
What I can do?
You and you and **Y-O-U**!

A, B, C, D,
E, F, G.
You can say it all with me.

H, I, J, K,
L, M, N, O, P.
I tell you, and you tell me.
Q, R, S, and T, U, V,
W, and X, Y, Z.

Now we can say the ABC.
We can go from A to Z.

47

The Big Box

A man put out a big box.
He put it out by his store.

Some boys came by.
"Boy!" they said.
"What a big box!"

They all jumped into the big box.

"A train!" one boy said.
"The box can be a train."

"Get on the train!" said the boys.

"Look," a boy said.
"The box can be a plane.
Come and ride on the plane!"

"Let's go!" the boys said.

"Look," said a boy.
"The box can be a good boat.
Get on the boat!"

"Let's go!" said the boys.

The boys went away.
The box was still by the store.

Three girls came by.
"Look at the big box," they said.
"Let's play in it."

The girls went into the box.
What could the box be now?

The box was not a boat.
It was not a train.
It was not a plane.

The box was a house.
And the girls played house all day.

"Scat, Cat!"

Not one boy was on the street.
And not one girl.

One car was on the street.
And one little cat.

The little cat went up the street.
She went down the street.

She was looking for some milk.

A man came over to the car.
The cat ran up to the man.

"Purr," said the little cat.
"Scat, cat!" the man said.
"SCAT!"

Then the man went away.
The cat was still looking for milk.

Then the cat saw a dog.
A woman was with the dog.
The cat ran up to the woman.

"Purr," said the little cat.
"G-r-r-r!" said the dog.
"Scat, cat!" said the woman.
"SCAT!"

The woman and the dog went away.
The cat was still looking for milk.

"Here, little cat.
Come here, cat," said a boy.

The cat saw the boy.
"Here, cat," said the boy.
"Here!"

The cat ran up the steps.
"Come in," said the boy.
"Come into my house."

The boy gave the cat some milk.

"Purr, purr," said the cat.

"Will you be my cat?" said the boy.

"Purr," said the little cat.
"Purr, purr, purr!"

One, Two, Three, Go!

"Let's run to the store," said Ken.
"O.K.," said Max.
"One, two, three, go!"

The boys ran down the street.
They ran fast.

60

A girl saw the boys running.
"What is it?" asked the girl.
"Come on!" said her friend.
"Let's run and see!"

The girls ran down the street.
They ran fast.

Some men saw the girls running.
"What is it?" asked one man.
His friend said, "Let's go see!"

The men ran down the street.
They ran fast.

A woman saw the men running.
"Is it a fire?" the woman asked.
"A fire?" asked her little girl.
"FIRE!" called a little boy.

People ran out of houses.
People ran out of stores.
They all ran down the street.
They all ran after the boys.

"I win!" called Ken.
"I win the race!"

"A race?" asked the little boy.
"A race?" asked the little girl.
"A race?" asked the woman.

"Yes," said one of the men.
"It was a race, not a fire."

"Come on," called Max.
"Let's race back.
See who wins now!"

"O.K.," said Ken.
"One, two, three, go!"

64

Part Three

The New Lunch Boxes

Ann had a new lunch box.
It was big and red.

Ken had a new lunch box.
It was big and red, too.
They had the lunch boxes at school.

The morning was over, and
Ken went to get his lunch box.

He looked in the box.
"This is not my lunch!" said Ken.

Ann went to get her lunch box.
She looked in the box.
"This is not my lunch!" said Ann.

The teacher came over.

The teacher looked at the boxes.

"Put your name on your lunch box,"
the teacher said to Ken.

"Put your name on your lunch box,"
the teacher said to Ann.

Ann did it.
Ken did it.

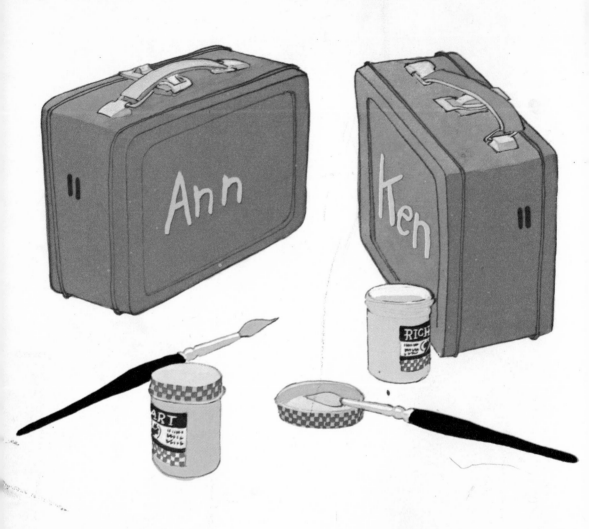

The boxes were still new and red.
But Ann could tell her lunch box
from Ken's lunch box.

And Ken could tell his lunch box
from Ann's lunch box.

And He Did!

One day, Henry saw a box
in the street.
"What a good box!" said Henry.

His friends came running.

"Who will help me get this box
over to my house?" Henry asked.

71

"Not I," said Ben.
"Not I," said Tony.
"Not I," said Ann.

"O.K., then," said Henry.
"I will get it there.
I will do it all by myself."

And he did.

But then there was work to do.
"Who will help me work
with the box?" Henry asked.

"Not I," said Ben.
"Not I," said Tony.
"Not I," said Ann.

"O.K., then," said Henry.
"I will do the work by myself."

And he did.

Henry had some skates.

"Who will help me put the skates on the box?" he asked.

"Not I," said Ben.
"Not I," said Tony.
"Not I," said Ann.

"O.K., then," said Henry.
"I will put the skates on the box all by myself."

And he did.

"Now who will have a ride?"
asked Henry.

"I will!" said Ben.
"I will!" said Tony.
"I will!" said Ann.

"You will not," said Henry.
"Not this time.
No, no, no.
This time, I will ride all by myself."

And he did!

Lunch on a Boat

One hot day, Roy went on a boat ride.
He went with his teacher and
his school friends.

It was cool on the water.
And it was fun.

The boat went by big city houses.
Slow boats and fast boats went by
in the water.
Roy saw a little boat pull
a big boat.

Then it was time for lunch.
Some children had lunch with them.
Some children had money
for hot dogs.
All the children had milk.

Roy had a hot dog.
His friend Max said,
"Look at the house boat, Roy."

Roy turned around fast.
His hot dog fell in the water.

"It fell!" said Roy.
"My hot dog fell.
Now I have no hot dog.
And I have no money."

"Here, Roy," said Max.
He gave some money to Roy.

"Thanks," said Roy.
He ran to get a new hot dog.

The children had a good ride
on the boat.

Then they came to the boat house.

"It was fun on the water," said a girl.

"It was cool, too," said the teacher.

"I liked my lunch on the boat,"
said a boy.

"I liked my hot dogs!" said Roy.

Jerry and the Girls

Jerry did not like girls.

When Jerry saw girls, he called,

"Look out! Here come the girls.

Let's get out of here!"

Some of Jerry's friends played
with girls.
But not Jerry!

Jerry always ran away.
He said, "I don't like girls!"

Some of Jerry's friends walked
to school with girls.
But not Jerry.

"You can walk to school with girls,"
said Jerry to his friends.
"But not me!"

Jerry always ran away
when his friends walked with girls.

One day Jerry's friends saw Jerry
walking with four girls.

"Can that be Jerry?" his friends
asked.

"Can that be Jerry walking
with four girls?"

Jerry walked over to his friends.

"What could I do?" Jerry said to them.

"My sister and her friends are going
to get some ice cream.

I am going with them.

I still don't like girls,
but do I like ice cream!"

City Houses

Molly and her father went out
for a walk.

They walked all the way
down the street.

"What is that?" asked Molly.

"The old houses are coming down,"
said her father.

"And then what?" asked Molly.

"A new house will go up,"
her father said.

"You will see."

Days went by.
Workmen came.
Trucks came.

More workmen came.
More trucks came.

Day after day, the men worked.
The new house went higher
and higher.

One day, Molly and her father
went out for a walk.
They walked all the way
down the street.

They saw the high, new house.
"That is the newest house
around here," said Molly.

"It is the newest now,"
said her father.

"But look over there."

Molly looked.
She saw more trucks.
The trucks stopped,
and workmen jumped down.
They went to work
on some more old houses.

90

Molly stopped to look at the men.
"Now what will they do?" she asked.

"A new house will go up there, too,"
said her father.
"Old houses come down.
New houses go up all the time
in the city."

Houses Up,
Houses Down

New houses go up in the city.
New houses go up in the town.
New houses go up in the city.
And the old, old houses come down.

The New Girl

Rosa came to live in the city.

Rosa walked down the steps
of the house.
"Hi," said a girl who lived
in the house, too.
"Are you the new girl?"

"No," said Rosa.
"I'm not new.
The city and this house are new."

93

Rosa went to the store
for her mother.

"Are you the new girl?"
asked the man in the store.

"No," said Rosa.
"I'm not new, but your store is new."

94

Then Rosa went to school.

"Here is the new girl,"
the teacher said.
"Her name is Rosa."

Rosa was going to say, "I'm not new.
Your school is new."

But she did not say it.

Rosa went to school all day
with all the girls and boys.

When the day was over,
the school was not so new.
The children were not so new.
Her house and the store
were not so new.
The city was not so new
to Rosa!

96

Part Four

The Big Snow

It snowed in the city.
Snow fell on the houses.
Snow fell on the cars.
Snow fell on the people.

Snow fell on all the streets.
Snow was high on the houses,
round on the cars.

More snow fell.
Cars and trucks were slow
in the snow.

Some cars and trucks could not go
at all.

They were stopped by the snow.

The children came out
to the street.

100

"Let's play in the snow,"
the children said.
"Let's make a snowman!"

The boys and girls made
a big snowman out in the street.
They worked on the snowman
all day.

In the night, the snow stopped.
A snowplow went down the street.
The snowplow pushed the snow
away.

It pushed the snowman down.

In the morning, the boys and girls came out.

"Where is the snowman?"
the children asked.

Then they saw the high snow
by the sidewalk.

One boy said, "The snowplow pushed
the snowman down."

"O.K., then," said a girl.
"Let's make a new snowman,
where the snowplow will not get it."

All that day, the boys and girls
worked in the snow.
They made a bigger snowman.
This time, they made the snowman
by the sidewalk.

No more snow fell in the city.
But the big snowman was there
for days and days.

Pete Makes a Friend

Pete had a new ball.
But Pete had no one to play with.

So he played by himself in the street.

The ball went fast.
The ball went high.

Then Pete made the ball go higher.
Up, up, up went Pete's new ball.
It went into a house!

Pete wanted to run away.
But he wanted his ball back, too.

He looked up at the house.
He saw a boy looking out.

"Hi," the boy called to Pete.
"Is this your ball?"

"Yes!" said Pete.

"O.K., here goes!" said the boy.

Now Pete had his ball back.
"Thanks," said Pete to the boy.
Then Pete said, "Can you
come out and play ball?"

The boy ran out of the house.
"My name is Victor," he said.
"My name is Pete," said Pete.

Pete and Victor played ball.

"Do you live in this house?"
Pete asked Victor.

"No, I don't," said Victor.
"My grandfather lives here.
I come over to see him."

Pete said, "I live over there."
"Say," said Victor, "I can call for you
when I come to see my grandfather.
Then we can play ball."

Now Pete had his ball
and a new friend, too.

City Policemen

All day and all night,
policemen walk.
 They walk up and down city streets.

 Policemen tell cars and trucks
when to stop.
 They tell people when to go.

Policemen ride on city streets.
They ride in police cars.
A policeman sees a car going too fast.
Ee-ee-ee-ee-ee!
The police car races after it.

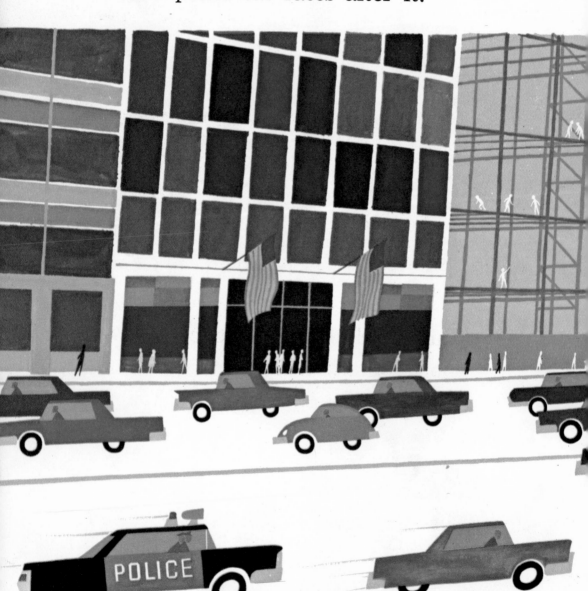

"Pull over!" calls the policeman.
The man stops his car.
"You were going too fast!"
says the policeman.

The man goes away in his car.
But this time, he goes slowly.

Policemen fly over the city, too!
They look down on the highways.

A car stops.
It can not go.
A policeman sees it.
He calls for help.

A truck comes.
A man works on the car.
Now the car can go.

Policemen ride in boats.

A policeman sees a man in the water.
The man calls, "Help!"

The police boat races over to help.
The policeman pulls the man
out of the water.

Policemen walk.
Policemen ride in cars.
They fly over the city.
They go in boats.
Policemen go all over the city,
by day and by night.

One Potato,
Two Potatoes

One day a little old woman
came walking in a little old town.
She had a big bag of potatoes.

But the bag fell down.

And out came the potatoes.
One potato,
Two potatoes,
Three potatoes,
Four.
Five potatoes,
Six potatoes,
Seven potatoes,
More!

Some potatoes rolled here.
Some potatoes rolled there.
They rolled all around
in the little old town.

Now the little old woman
had no potatoes.
They had all rolled away.
Down.
Down.
Down.

A boy came walking.
A girl came walking.
A man came walking, too.
They all had potatoes.

And they all gave the potatoes
back to the little old woman.

"Thank you, one and all,"
said the little old woman.

Then away she went, with
One potato,
Two potatoes,
Three potatoes,
Four.
Five potatoes,
Six potatoes,
Seven potatoes,
More!

The Tugboat

Many people were on a big boat.
The boat was going away
from the city, out to sea.

But the boat was so big
that it could not turn by itself.

A little tugboat came to help
the big boat.

The tugboat pulled and pulled.
Slowly, the big boat turned.

The little tugboat turned the big boat
around in the water.

"Good-by!" the people called.
"Good-by, good-by.
Have a good time!"

The tugboat pulled the big boat.

Away went the little tugboat
with the big boat in the water.

After this, the big boat could go
by itself.

So the little tugboat turned and
came back to the city.

And the big boat went out to the sea.

VOCABULARY LIST

Around the City

Around the City, the Primer of the Bank Street Basal Reading series, introduces 164 new words. Regular inflections of known words formed by adding the endings *s*, *ed*, and *ing* are not counted as new words; when the inflected form has been introduced first, the root word is not counted as a new word. All 29 of these words have been starred.

7.	39. Carmen	68. teacher	95.
8. around	could	69. your	96. so
town	went	name	were
9. play	still	70. Ken's	97.
10.	friend*	71. Henry	98. snow
11. hot	40. box	help	snowed*
12. sit	mail	72. Tony	99. round
steps	41. wash	there	100.
13. water	42. grandmother	myself	101. snowman
cool	43. milk	73.	make
sits*	44. did	74. skates	made
14.	45. wet	75. no	102. snowplow
15. but	46. can	time	pushed
16. too	47. tell	76. Roy	103. where
likes	we	77. pull	sidewalk
do	48. by	boats*	104. bigger
like*	came	78. them	105. days*
you	said	money	106. Pete
17. dog	49. be	children	ball
18. jump	train	dogs*	himself
fun	jumped*	79. fell	107.
me	50. plane	thanks	108. wanted
19.	51. let's	turned*	109.
20. get	boat	80. liked	110. Victor
ride	52. was	81. Jerry	111. grandfather
sees*	53.	when	him
21. from	54. scat	82. always	112. call*
jumps*	cat	don't	113. policemen
22. slow	car*	83. walked	114. police
fast	55. looking*	walk*	policeman
23. looks*	for	84. walking*	115. slowly
24. his	56. ran	that	calls*
step*	purr	four	116. highways
25.	57. saw	85. sister	117. races*
26.	woman	am	pulls*
27. rides*	58. here	going*	118.
28. after	59. gave	86. Molly	119. potato
what	60. Ken	way	potatoes
29. with	O.K.	87. coming	bag
my	Max	old	120. five
30. friends	61. running	88. workmen	six
TV	asked	higher	seven
31.	men	more	121. rolled
32. drill	62. called	worked*	122.
ring	of	89. newest	123.
33. little	63. win	90. stopped	124. tugboat
big	race	91.	sea
34. talk	64. wins*	92.	itself
not	65.	93. Rosa	turn*
35. then	66. boxes	live	125. pulled*
now	new	I'm	126.
36. rooms*	had	lived	127.
37.	67. this	94.	
38. rained	looked*